THE SHEEP
AND THE
ROWAN TREE

Written and illustrated by

Julia Butcher

Holt, Rinehart and Winston
New York

First published in the United States in 1984 by
Holt, Rinehart and Winston, 383 Madison Avenue,
New York, New York 10017.
Originally published in Great Britain
by Methuen Children's Books Ltd.

Library of Congress Cataloging in Publication Data

Butcher, Julia.
The sheep and the rowan tree.

Summary: A discontented rowan tree learns to appre-
ciate its position more after being visited by a well-
traveled bird, who tells it how unsuitable it would be to live
anywhere else.
[1. Trees—Fiction] I. Title.
PZ7.B969Sh 1984   [E]   83-26423

ISBN: 0-03-071602-0
First American Edition
Printed in Great Britain
1 3 5 7 9 10 8 6 4 2

ISBN 0-03-071602-0

AUTHOR'S NOTE

*The rowan tree is found on hills and mountains
throughout Europe and North America. It thrives in cold climates and
is known for its beautiful red berries
and small white flowers.*

nce upon a time, there was a beautiful rowan tree. It grew in the middle of a big grassy field. When the sun was high in the sky, a flock of sheep came to rest in the shade of the tree.

hen it rained, the sheep sought shelter under the leafy branches.

ometimes the sheep wandered away to a pine tree on the far side of the field, while the lambs chased each other across the grass. The rowan tree also longed to see new places. It was tired of being rooted to the same spot.

ne day, a large blue bird flew down and landed on the top of the rowan tree. The migrating bird had lost its way in a storm and was far off course.

he bird told the rowan tree about its home in a far-off land, and the rowan tree told the bird of its longing to see different places. Because the bird had traveled nearly all the way around the world, it was able to describe other lands to the tree.

here are many trees and different kinds of animals in the tropical forests,' said the bird, 'but your little branches could not reach the sunlight, and you would be choked by the undergrowth.'

n the desert there is plenty of sunshine,' said the bird, 'but it hardly ever rains, so there are no clouds to hide the sun.'

he polar regions would be cooler,' said the bird, 'but there it is winter all the time, and your leaves would fall off, never to grow again.'

oral islands are beautiful when the sea is calm,' said the bird, 'but when there are hurricanes, you could not bend with the wind and the waves of the sea would splash you with salty water.'

**S**ome people have very pretty gardens,' said the bird, 'but they would pick your flowers, make jelly with your berries, and trim your leaves.'

here are many big cities in the world where you might grow very well,' said the bird, but children would swing on your branches and carve their names on your trunk.'

his field is just right for you,' said the bird. 'Here you have a little sunshine, a little rain, and some very good friends. Now that I have rested awhile, I must continue my journey.' Then the bird flew high up into the sky.

The rowan tree was very unhappy to have lost the beautiful blue bird. The sheep were very unhappy because the pine tree they were living under wasn't shady enough.

o the sheep returned to their favorite tree and at last the rowan tree knew that it had already found the best place to live in the whole wide world.